For my three princes and little princess:
Noah, Milo, Zen and Lotus, and for my mom
Katharyn and my sister Nefeterius

www.theenglishschoolhouse.com

Copyright © 2021 by Dr. Tamara Pizzoli

ISBN: 978-1-955130-02-8

TWELVE ABYSSINIAN PRINCESSES

By Dr. Tamara Pizzoli - Illustrated by Elena Tommasi Ferroni

In the East African city of Hora Finfinne, quite some time ago--in a land that was once called Abyssinia but is now known as Ethiopia, there lived a stately king, his gorgeous wife, the queen, and their twelve remarkable daughters:

Liya, Aida, Zala, Maaza, Marjani, Kamali, Ife, Zoya, Nuru, Bathsheba, Faiza and Habiba.

Now these twelve daughters ranged in size from teeny to tall, and though their interests varied, one thing the half-dozen had in common was their affinity for both shoes and dancing.

The King was of serious character, and quite strict. Thus, he insisted that his daughters leave home only if absolutely necessary.

"Every whim and wonder they could ever want is right here in this palace." the King would say, and he made sure it was so.

Though he loved his daughters dearly, the masses of slippers, sandals,wedges and heels they left strewn about the palace got on his very last royal nerve...

and then there was the music.

Why the King and Queen could barely greet each other

or the day without having to shout over a loud instrument of some sort.

They couldn't get a word in edge-wise while trying to converse over lunch.

And it was nearly impossible for the royal couple to get a sound night of sleep.

As the princesses grew, so did the noise, and it was becoming too much

for the King and Queen to comfortably bear.

The Queen sighed and began, "Why don't we grant the princesses permission to dance just for one night...outside, altogether? They are older now. What harm or trouble could come to them?"

The King was silent for some time before he finally nodded and agreed.

Upon hearing the news, the princesses could hardly believe their luck! They spent the better part of the day primping, preparing and posing in their party attire.

"Be back before midnight," the Queen advised her daughters as she braided her hair.

"Mother," the eldest daughter Aida smiled,
"Who do you take us for? Cinderella?"
Her sisters giggled as the Queen retired to her room.
Once their mother was out of sight, the princesses carefully set
every clock in the house back by six hours.

That evening, Liya, Aida, Zala, Maaza, Marjani, Kamali, Ife, Zoya, Nuru, Bathsheba, Faiza and Habiba were accompanied by a chauffeur to the grandest ball in the land.

The princesses whirled and twirled the night away without worry or care, as they'd all but stopped time at the palace. They danced until the soles of their shoes wore thin.

Meanwhile, the King waited in the grand reception room for his daughters to return.

He relaxed on his favorite chair, and though he tried to fight succumbing to a slumber, he simply could not manage to stay awake.

To be sure he didn't miss his daughters' arrival, and because he had a sneaky suspicion that the dozen would not make it home before curfew, the King gathered every pot and pan that he could find in the kitchen, and stacked them all high against the front door.

With that he returned to his chaise, and within three minutes he was fast asleep.

The princesses arrived home late that night, each one on tiptoe. Aida, the eldest, eased the front door of the palace open as quietly as she could, and just as she gave the slightest push, a huge clatter rang out that could have easily awakened everyone in the home:

PING!

POW! BOOM!

BAM! KATANG!

TINNNNNNNG!

The King woke up with a start and jumped to his feet.
"I knew it!" he cried! "You all are late! What time is it?"

The princesses shrugged as the King glanced at the clock nearby.
He could hardly believe his eyes.
The princesses had made it home, with plenty of time to spare,
yet the sun was just starting her ascent into the sky.

The next day, the princesses pleaded with their parents to let them attend another ball and dance just once more.
But the King and the Queen both agreed their daughters had enjoyed
 enough fun to last for quite some time.

That evening, the sisters gathered as sisters do,
and talked as sisters talk,
and planned as sisters plan.

And that very night, while their father slept peacefully after a meal of kitfo, gomen and rice and their mother braided her hair,
the twelve princesses slipped away in pairs and snuck out into the darkness.

Now who exactly paddled the boat that held the twelve princesses
across the mote just outside their palace is not known.

Surely the dozen were full of both charm and coins,
both of which helped to secure the fare.

They arrived to an event even more splendid than the one they attended the night before.

Right away they began having a ball.

Back at the palace, the King and Queen both tossed and turned constantly. Neither one could get a wink of sleep. The palace was quiet...
too quiet.

The royal couple shared first a knowing feeling, and then a knowing glance.

Silently the Queen began to unravel her braids as the King dressed in his regal attire.

An hour later, the King and Queen stood and watched their daughters solemnly at the entrance of the grand ball.

There they were:

Liya, Aida, Zala, Maaza, Marjani, Kamali, Ife, Zoya, Nuru, Bathsheba, Faiza and Habiba, whirling and twirling about as if it were their business to do so.

It wasn't until the Master of Ceremonies announced to the crowd that it was an immense honor to have the King and the Queen in attendance that the princesses screeched to a halt.

The rest of the ballroom followed suit.

The princesses could feel the heat of their parents' anger from across the room.

No words were needed as the dozen formed a single file and headed toward the nearest exit with their chins slightly lowered.

The Master of Ceremonies, desperate to have the royal family stay just a bit longer, orchestrated a rousing rendition of the Queen's favorite song.

First, Her Majesty's hair began to sway, then her head and neck, followed by her shoulders and arms.

Soon she had cleared the dance floor with her rhythm and joy.
She summoned for her husband to join her.

And he did.

And together, the King and Queen danced the night away and greeted the new day with their souls warm and their shoe soles worn.

In fact, it was the twelve princesses who had to make their parents leave the ball.

And from that day forth, The King added three new responsibilities to his royal title:

Choreographer, Chaperone, and Chauffeur.